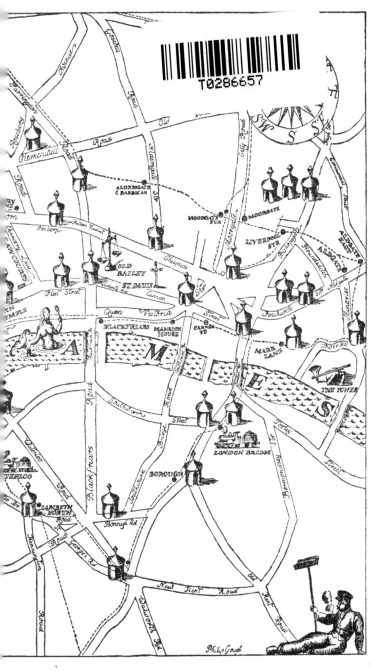

FOR YOUR
CONVENIENCE

First published . . *1937*

Printed in Great Britain by T. and A. CONSTABLE LTD.
at the University Press, Edinburgh

FOR YOUR CONVENIENCE

A learned Dialogue,
Instructive to all Londoners
& London Visitors, Overheard
in the Thélème Club and
Taken down Verbatim

BY

Paul Pry

Published by

**GEORGE ROUTLEDGE
& SONS LTD**

Broadway House

68-74 Carter Lane E.C.

1937

First published by George Routledge and Sons 1937
This edition published by Muswell Press in 2019

Every effort has been made to trace the owner of the rights for
the artwork by Philip Gough but this has proved impossible. The
publisher would be glad to hear from the copyright holder.

Printed and bound by CPI Group (UK) Ltd, CR0 4YY

A CIP catalogue record for this book is
available from the British Library

ISBN: 9781999313555

Muswell Press
London N6 5HQ
www.muswell-press.co.uk

FOR YOUR CONVENIENCE

"NO, sir," growled Mr. Mumble, Doyen of the Théléme Club; "no, sir, I have *not* done with the *Sanitary World and Drainage Observer*. And what the hell do you want with it, anyway?"

"I beg your pardon, sir," said the young new member, with the courtesy due to grey hairs that is so prominent in modern youth ; " I beg your pardon, sir. But I have read all the periodicals on the Magazine Table, and a lousy lot they are. Seeing you so engrossed in the *Sanitary World and Drainage Observer*, I jumped to the conclusion that perhaps one paper in the club had something interesting in it, and when you laid it aside——"

" It contains nothing interesting to the layman, young man. At least, so far as I can see. I had laid it aside only to prepare for another combing of its columns. I had hoped from its title that it might tell one some of the things a man often wants to know. But so far as my first examination goes, it does not."

" Such things as what, may one ask ? "

" Why, sir, from its title one would judge that it would tell one what to do if one were walking through Wigmore Street after three cups of tea—a predicament that presented itself to me yesterday afternoon. But it does not."

"I get you, sir," said the young man amiably. "I get you. But to the habitual and observant peregrinator of the London streets, Wigmore Street presents little difficulty."

"I say it does, sir. A great deal. Wigmore Street — why, that street, under different names, stretches from Tottenham Court Road to Edgware Road. It begins as Goodge Street, continues as Mortimer Street, changes to Cavendish Place, then becomes Wigmore Street, and later Seymour Street. I have not paced it with surveying instruments, but I should judge it to be about a mile and a half in length. And in the whole stretch, not one place for a gentleman. Or even a man."

"Nevertheless, sir," persisted the young man, "Wigmore Street presents little difficulty. The other sections, yes, but not the Wigmore Street section—when you know."

"And what should I have known?"

"Why, sir, St. Christopher's Place —that engaging little passage at the middle of the street, full of antique shops and second-hand bookshops. In a cul-de-sac at the end of that passage you would have found full service, with bright railings round it. And in a street on the right, just below Marylebone Lane and going towards Portman Square—in that street is a public yard provided with one of those zinc or iron enclosures painted a grateful green."

"Well, well, well. You seem remarkably informed on Wigmore Street."

"Not only on Wigmore Street, sir, but on many another. Indeed, I may say that I have made a study of this recondite matter. And necessarily, since my favourite drink is either Pilsner or Münchner."

"Pilsner or Münchner—ha! Fresh

and flavoursome drinks, both of them. When I was younger I indulged in them myself, both here and in their native cities. But that was in days when the word renal conveyed nothing to me. What is your customary allowance of these wholesome beverages ? "

" Why, sir, I do not partake with the freedom of the German student. But at midday I usually manage to Knock Back half a doz——"

" Knock Back ? "

" Ah, sir, you must pardon my careless use of the crude terminology of to-day. To Knock Back—to defeat, to demolish, to consume. Yes, at midday I usually manage to Knock Back half a dozen of the best, and in the evenings perhaps some nine or ten."

" Indeed. In that case your interest in the matter that led me to consult this journal is easily comprehended."

" Quite, sir. You see, while the authorities of London look after its people on the whole in the most admirable and thoughtful fashion, in this particular matter they are a little shy. All other services and amenities are easily found. Post - offices, police - stations, fire - stations, swimming - baths, taxi - ranks—these are obvious, or their situation may easily be located by the help of the Telephone Book. But, apart from the main streets, this other matter is left to individual and accidental discovery. I have now, however, acquired a knowledge not only of this matter, but of various ins-and-outs of London with which I frequently confound those who claim to know their city. I believe there is a school for taxi-drivers called the Knowledge of London School. I wonder whether its professors could name off-hand the situation of the nearest necessary station from this point or that?"

"I should doubt it," said Mr. Mumble. "The subject has not yet received the attention it deserves, and there is no general clearing-house for information upon it. Even local people I have found deficient in such necessary knowledge. Tell me, what would you do if caught in, say, Bayswater Road after—to adapt a Keats title—After Leaving Some Friends at a Late Hour . . . forgetfully ? "

" Why, sir, as a young man, I should make but a small matter of vaulting the rails of Kensington Gardens. But with elder men that performance would be out of the question. Bayswater Road . . . yes, you set me a problem there. The stretch from Marble Arch to Notting Hill Gate is certainly a barren stretch. But stay—just off Queen's Road, if I remember, there is a mews, or garage, where an enclosure may be found."

" That is worth knowing. Portland Place is another awkward spot."

" Yes, indeed," the young man assented. " Curious, isn't it, that one of the worst-served districts in this matter should be the medical district ? All round there—Portland Place, Devonshire Street, Queen Anne Street, Wimpole Street, Weymouth Street, Harley Street—where you would think there would be adequate provision for the body's needs, there is indeed little. Though perhaps in those streets, full of practitioners and specialists dealing every day in kindred matters, one could knock at any door without giving offence by one's request.

" From Oxford Circus to the end of Portland Place is a stretch in which the stranger certainly would find himself in a dilemma. And, as I say, he would only increase it by searching any of the streets east or west. But at the end, if he continues round Park Crescent, he will come into Marylebone Road, where he may find a station at the junction of Great Portland Street and Euston Road."

" I shall make a note of that. Increasing age often takes me into that district."

"Kensington," continued the young man, "is another difficult district. It is true that it has many public-houses, but, as a rule in London, those that have outside offices are ungenerous enough to close them when the house itself is closed. So that for many hours of the day they are but *ignis fatui*. And it has tube-stations, but nothing on the surface. One has to take a ticket and descend to the platform."

"Ah, yes, I have encountered that. Being once in some unease in Tottenham Court Road, I entered Goodge Street tube-station, and enquired of a porter. He told me they had once had such a place on the surface, but that it was closed—because it got abused. Often in wakeful hours I have pondered that remark, but it has never clarified itself."

"Why, sir, I think I perceive his meaning. You see, places of that kind which have no attendants afford excellent rendezvous to people who wish to meet out of doors and yet escape the eye of the Busy. Such people as street-bookmakers, who can there meet their clients and pass their slips. Or crooks who wish to exchange information out of earshot of their friends or the observation of the Dicks."

" The Busy ? The Dicks ? " said Mr. Mumble.

" Why, yes—the police—detectives —plain-clothes men."

" Indeed ? It seems to me, young man, that you know far too many things a gentleman should not know."

" That may be, sir. And it may be that if I go on talking I shall give you further evidence of my wide knowledge of things that matter. Though who is the arbiter on what should and should not be known, I cannot guess. I thought Lord Chesterfield died in the late eighteenth century."

" He did, sir. More's the pity. But continue."

" Well, sir, I choose to ignore Lord

Chesterfield and to take all knowledge to be my providence—as a far greater man than Lord Chesterfield did. And though some of that knowledge may, as you imply, be homespun, even a trifle shabby, you've no idea how often it has proved useful to me. As in the matter we are discussing. When, for instance, I have been at a loss in Dalston, in Streatham, in Clerkenwell, in Bermondsey—knowledge acquired on previous journeys has been a blessing."

" But how, young man, do you come to know these populous but unfrequented districts. What took you there ? "

" Why, sir, my first job, on leaving the Secondary School, was that of travelling in tap-washers for the old firm of——"

" On leaving the *what* ? "

" On leaving the Secondary School."

" The Sec—— The *Secondary* School ? Secondary School ? What the hell are you doing in the Thélème Club ? Who let you in ? "

" Well, sir, I was duly proposed and seconded in the usual course; and I was elected by a majority—nay, by the unanimous voice—of the Committee."

" Good God in Heaven ! What shall we hear next ? Secondary School ! And a member of the Thélème ! Psfchtzz ! "

" Why, sir, you must know that times change. And customs with them."

" So it seems. They do indeed. Secondary School — chrrffpff ! No wonder you are informed about these things and about such things as Busies. The Thélème, and the——"

" Well, sir, the fact that my father had not sufficient money to send me to one of those schools which alone give one the right to call oneself an Englishman—surely that, sir, reflects rather on his business capacity than on my social or moral character. And reflects, too, on the stupidity of his great-great-grandfathers in not, like the ancestors of so many members of this club, founding a family fortune by playing pimp or money-lender to some prince. However, since my presence is distasteful . . ."

" No, no," said Mr. Mumble hurriedly. " I did not suggest that. By no means. Far from it. Do sit down. I find you, on the contrary, a personable and most knowledgeable young fellow, and far better mannered than most of the young members here. No, no—I should never have connected you with a Secondary School had you not told me."

" Whether that is a compliment I cannot determine, not knowing how you visualize the scholars of Secondary Schools. A certain inflection of voice, to say nothing of your exclamations——"

" No matter, young man, no matter. I am sometimes inclined to be hasty. All I will say now is that, Secondary

School or no Secondary School, I find that your talk, unlike that of most of the younger members here, is more than monosyllables. Is, indeed, at times, almost interesting."

" It has ever been my endeavour to make it so. Hence my researches after curious knowledge."

" Pray continue, then, pray continue. And perhaps you will join me in a seidel of your favourite beverage, and expunge in it my hasty remarks. Shall it be light or dark ? "

" Light, I think," said the young man ; " though in the end 'tis all one. Like the life of man, it presents us with a few moments of bliss, and then returns whence it came, to return once again from the moist earth as corn or grain or root, to repeat the process. Let it be Pilsner."

" Very well. I myself must be contented with a lithia water. . . . You were saying, I think . . ."

" Ah, yes. . . . Permit me to Knock

this Back. To you, sir. Here's looking towards you, and another kind love,
and may your closing years be of an
argent serenity, with no regrets for
delicious things you might have done
and were restrained by conscience from
doing. . . . Yes, as I was saying, on
leaving the Secondary School I became
traveller to the old, even aged, firm of
Dogsbody and Doolittle, makers of tap-
washers. As my duties took me into
remote corners of London, and as I had
already acquired my enduring taste for
the brews of Bavaria and Czecho-Slo-
vakia, it became necessary for me to
acquaint myself with all opportunities
for personal comfort. How often, in
the early days, did I wander about a
forlorn district, looking for the blessed
word, when all the time (as, by acci-
dent, I would learn next day) I had
been within ten yards of the desired
but hidden haven."

"Most irritating," said Mr. Mumble.
"The situation comes home to me. In

certain Latin countries, of course, these things are better done. There, almost every few yards, or so it seems, has its zinc surround. And in one or two cities, church walls and even cathedral walls afford service. They have no timidity in this matter. In Brussels, before they show you the Hôtel de Ville and St. Gudule, they are most anxious that you should see a certain small public statue. But here, as you say, these things are occult—only to be lit upon by haphazard steps."

" As the fruit of long investigation," went on the young man, " I now have in preparation a series of section-plans of the London streets, suitable for the pocket, on which I am marking with a green dot the precise location of every refuge. I shall, of course, present a set to the club library, and if you, sir, will accept a personal set——"

" That is kind of you. It will be most useful—one of those little things, long-needed, of which the need is never fully realized until it is supplied. And the green dots should give it a pleasing appearance. Some time ago, I saw a catalogue of the publications of the L.C.C., and in it I found an item, The Main Drainage of London, with Illustrations and a Map of Sewers. I sent for a copy, but it contained nothing of the kind I wanted. There is Oxford Street, for example . . ."

" Yes. Certainly there appears to be nothing between Oxford Circus and the Marble Arch. But, none the less, there are certain bolt-holes. There are the many big stores, in which one may pass as a potential customer and share in their amenities—if one is prepared to take a lift-journey to the oomth floor. And tents may be found in the mews, or garages, around South Molton Street and Brook Street. In the section between Oxford Circus and Tottenham Court Road, places may be found at the bottom of Argyll Street; in a little court at the end of Rathbone Place; and at

the end of a little court running between Newman Street and Little
Goodge Street.

"Chancery Lane looks bare to the
eye, and suggests that one may have to
journey up to Holborn, and seek the
refuge in the road by the Prudential
Insurance office, or down to Fleet
Street, and seek either the place at the
bottom of Fetter Lane or the place by
St. Clement Danes. But Chancery
Lane does offer help—in the little turn-
ing opposite Bream's Buildings."

"Your wanderings have indeed been
productive. But how about St. John's
Wood?"

"Ah, there I fear you have me. A
benighted and troublesome district,
that. And those long roads—Abbey
Road, Grove End Road, Loudoun Road,
Avenue Road, Wellington Road, Ade-
laide Road. Indeed, between Lord's
and Swiss Cottage I fear my map must
be blank. Though, of course, I have
not fully completed my survey, and a

further visit to the district may enable me to chart it. It is a district to which business never took me—tap-washers, for some reason, being longer lived in some parts of London than others. Marylebone High Street was one of my districts, and that street, and its continuation, Thayer Street — the two stretching from Marylebone Road to Manchester Square — is another bad spot to be caught in. The only relief is to be found in one side-street, Paradise Street, I think it is, near the old burial-ground."

" I must try to remember that."

" It may be useful to you, sir, to remember that when seeking a refuge away from the main streets, it is a good general rule to look about for a yard. It is in yards that the authorities tuck them. Why, I cannot say. It is not that they are shy of offering the service itself, for when they do it really well—a spacious place below ground, with an attendant, and bright fixtures by Doulton, and green railings, or, in the City of Westminster, silver railings —then they plank it in everybody's view, with numerous signs and labels. As in the middle of Regent Street—in the full light of Leicester Square—in the middle of Knightsbridge—in the busy and populous Cambridge Circus—in the road between the Garrick Theatre and the Portrait Gallery—visible to natives and foreigners. But when the product is only a green enclosure, the authorities seem to become bitter and shamefaced about it. Possibly this reflects some dissatisfaction with the design, or some other aesthetic revulsion. Certainly they do hide these places in corners that nobody but local inhabitants, or prying adventurers like myself, would know about. So always look for a yard.

" In France, as we agree, it is done differently. There, whatever the style or size, whether a real building or a mere enclosure, it is treated in the same way, and is placed unshamedly in main streets, clear to the general view. And, lest the traveller even so should miss it, it is marked with signs which by long usage have become associated with it, almost, indeed, synonyms for it. Your sure guide in Paris is Chocolat Menier or Amer Picon.

" In the provincial towns of England, a safe tip is to look for a statue of Queen Victoria. Wherever you see that, you may be pretty sure that a refuge is near by, if not, as often happens, right at the august feet. In other places, the Town Hall is a reliable beacon. Or sometimes the statue of the local money-grubber who, in his old age, gave away what he didn't want and built the Free Library and the Swimming Bath. In return for which, the Town Council puts him in his place."

" It is certainly odd," said Mr. Mumble, " that our attitude to the matter should be what it is. In this country it can scarce ever be mentioned; or, when mentioned, is treated as something not for the open ear. Yet it was not always so with us. In older times we English were as frank towards it as the Latins or the Teutons. Even if we did isolate it from other things by making a jest of it. In the eighteenth century, and even the early nineteenth, no man needed to suffer, since public decorum was not then so easily disturbed. People were not so aware of *pudibonderie*."

"Quite," said the young man. "From my own eighteenth-century reading—necessarily much less comprehensive than yours, sir—but from Ned Ward, Swift, Gay, Smollett, Fielding, and others, one gathers that means were taken at times of necessity without regard to municipal provision—or the lack of it. Though as to the early nineteenth century, I do recall an anecdote showing high susceptibility

on the part of Long's Hotel—that used
to be in Bond Street. And that, despite
the fact that the person concerned was
a lord, which in the early nineteenth
century meant something."

" What anecdote was that ? "

" Why, sir, it runs that no less a
person than Lord Byron was barred
from Long's Hotel after a certain inci-
dent. Which centred on the point that
on a cold wet night Lord Byron deemed
the hall to be a less inclement place
than an uncovered yard."

" H'm. . . . There, I think, I am with
the hotel. After all, in a busy hotel.
. . . But have your wanderings taken
you much to the City ? Once or twice,
on visits to my stockbroker, I have
been at a loss, and——"

" Yes, I know the City pretty well,
and it does, as you say, present some
difficulty to the stranger. And then,
things change so rapidly there. Even
in my short experience, many a useful
spot has disappeared. There might be

a court or a yard where one knew that service was to be had. After a lapse of maybe three weeks, one looks for it, and lo, rebuilding operations have begun, the yard is razed, the place is gone, and it is not re-born elsewhere. None the less, a little research shows that the City is well provided."

" Another seidel, young man ? "

" I will, sir. These light beverages digest themselves easily and rapidly. . . . Grant me a moment's absence. . . .

" Now, sir, peace, health and freedom from climatic draughts and over-drafts. . . . The City, yes. Cheapside, for example, appears to be served only at the point where it meets St. Martin's-le-Grand, or at the subway at the Mansion House end. But go down King Street, and alongside the Guild-hall, in a byway called Guildhall Build-ings, a refuge will be found. Also in the Guildhall itself, off the Reading Room. Again, friends of mine have complained to me of being in difficulties in Gracechurch Street and Leadenhall Street. I direct them to step into Leadenhall Market and enquire for Lime Street Passage. Fenchurch Street has nothing until nearly its eastern end, but there you find not only a public place, at the corner of London Street, but also Fenchurch Street Station. Places here, of course, are not so numerous as in other parts of town, since the major population is engaged in offices, each of which has its own arrangements. And every square yard of City territory is so valuable that it is used, wherever possible, for buildings that are productive. Green enclosures are little seen, if at all. The labouring quarters, near the river, are perhaps the best served. Such quarters as Upper and Lower Thames Street and round about the Tower ; also, among the warehouses at the back of Wood Street—such as Fore Street, part of London Wall, and Red Cross Street. As a note for an emergency, you might remember that many of the very large blocks of office buildings have places in their basements, which, like those of New York and other American cities, are available not only to the minor staffs of the different offices, but to casual callers who may or may not have business in the building."

"Useful information," said Mr. Mumble. "It is related of Herbert Spencer, with whose acquaintance I was honoured in his latter years, when he was somewhat uncommunicative and three-parts deaf, but as stimulating as ever ; it is said that, being unable to play the game of billiards, he remarked, in a moment of envy which sat ill upon a philosopher, that proficiency at billiards was evidence of a misspent youth. What term he would attach to your proficiency in the particular sphere you have made your own, I cannot guess. Possibly, as a man of sense, he would applaud it and consider that it represented time not ill-spent. But as a synthetic philosopher he might——"

"You must remember, sir, that my knowledge was acquired incidentally, during the time when I was extremely active on the behalf of Messrs. Dogsbody and Doolittle—and of course my own. It just came to me, ancillary to my long daily travels. And in so far as it is useful to myself and to others, no philosopher, I think, could call it vain. And by the way, sir, eminent as Herbert Spencer may have been in Philosophy, his remark about billiards shows superficial observation. Many of the best men I have taken on did not begin until they were thirty. It is, after all, a game for the steady and contemplative temperament, for the leisurely step and quiet eye—which seldom go with nineteen or twenty."

"I fancy you're right. I myself did not indulge until I was over forty, and in a couple of years I could show quite a reasonable game against some of the youngsters. But about the City . . .''

" Well, I don't know that I can say much more about that. If I add such spots as Liverpool Street and Broad Street Stations ; Bishopsgate, outside Dirty Dick's; the Bank subway; King William Street, at Gracechurch Street corner ; Cannon Street Station ; the corner of Lothbury and Moorgate Street, behind the Bank ; the junction of Queen Victoria Street and Cannon Street ; the western end of Cheap-side ; and Newgate Street, by the Old Bailey—you will see, I think, from your knowledge of the City, that its places, though few, are not far distant from one another."

" Now how about those unfriendly tracts you have mentioned, such as Kensington, St. John's Wood, and so on ? In an emergency, how do you proceed ? "

" Why, sir, in many districts, otherwise ill-served, you have large hotels.

St. John's Wood, unfortunately, has none, but in Bloomsbury, the West End, and parts of Kensington, they are often salvation. One can always saunter in and ask for the hairdresser's department. Again, police-stations and fire-stations in those barren districts are usually well disposed to a polite request. Many a time, in my tap-washer days, I found them of service, and a few words of thanks and a little chat made one free of them for other occasions.

" It is from chats of that kind, if you are curious to know, that I came to learn about Busies. And, among many other things, about the etiquette observed between the local fire-engine at a fire, and the outlying engines called in to assist. Garages, too, are usually ready to accede to any courteously-worded appeal. Indeed, the only places where you are received with a shudder of recoil — though, truthfully, I only once made such an approach — are private houses. . . . Of the many awkward tracts the most awkward are those groups of squares, as in Bayswater and Bloomsbury, Belgravia and Pimlico. In Bloomsbury, between Tottenham Court Road and Southampton Row, I know of nothing. Nor in the Row itself, save, as I say, the hotels. Nothing, indeed, save at the end of the Row, by Theobald's Road, or way down Guilford Street, where it meets Lamb's Conduit Street. Going north up the Row, beyond Tavistock Square, you have, I think, nothing until Camden Town, unless you turn aside into Euston Station.

"Edgware Road is another. But the length between Marble Arch and Harrow Road, each point offering service, is not great, and it is hardly necessary to do as a friend of mine, ignorant of the district, did in an emergency that occurred in Cambridge Terrace. All he could think of was to take a taxi to Paddington. From

Harrow Road and along Maida Vale
you have nothing that I can be sure of
until you come to the beginning of
Kilburn; though I seem to remember
a yard off Clifton Road."

"Strange," mused Mr. Mumble ;
"strange that we, created and builded
so wonderfully, should yet be subject
to having our momentary affairs over-
thrown by such ungainly occasions.
It was that, I think, that made Swift
so irreconcilable to the idea of man's
majesty. The subject recurs in both
his verse and his prose. And of course
Rabelais found it often a useful re-
minder wherewith to rock man's pride
in himself. There is room there, I
fancy, for a thoughtful paper for the
Untrodden Paths Review, to which
I sometimes send a little study or dis-
sertation on some overlooked corner of
man's story. I will perhaps devote a
few wet afternoons to it, of course
with acknowledgments to yourself as
being its inspiration."

"Speaking of inspiration, sir, I have often been struck—and doubtless you have—with the curiosa to which some people are inspired in such places. Particularly in the limerick form. It is matter for investigation that this form, an innocent form, employed by Edward Lear for childish jingles—as innocent, indeed, as the rondeau, the villanelle, or the chant-royal—it is certainly odd that this form should lend itself more effectively than any other to the perpetration and release of all that is indecorous."

"True," said Mr. Mumble. "I must give my mind to it. It might produce a very choice piece for the *Untrodden Paths Review*."

"From a study of these scribblings," went on the young man, "one learns that the restless imp that moved in Bardolph and Launce and Sir John, and in Rochester and Sedley, has not yet been quieted. This body of literature, which one cannot call unwritten

but may call unperceived—at least by
the majority—persists and grows. It
is the irrepressible demand for the
abolition of tabu. Its other why's and
wherefore's may afford study to the
Groddecks and Kraft-Ebings of to-day.
For myself, I prefer merely to recog-
nize it, and to see in it an attempt,
by ridicule, to make men ashamed of
being ashamed of the things they are
ashamed of."

" To me," said Mr. Mumble, " it
appears more as a manifestation of the
undying *cochon*. Which grew, maybe,
from man's bitter recognition that when
all is said and thought, he remains kin
with the brutes ; a recognition that is
keener in those places than elsewhere.
He can be angelic. And he can be
Caliban. But at his best, he is still
no more than the divine animal. Yet
his recognition of this should not be
bitter. He must shed this attitude,
and, as Groddeck says (it is part of your
interest, young man, that you should

mix knowledge of Busies and of the London byways with knowledge of Groddeck), as he says, man will not be free until he does this."

"Quite. I read the three Groddeck works a year or so ago."

"And I heard him lecture, and at the time I wished I hadn't, and when I thought it over next day, I was glad I had. . . . Reverting to the literature of walls. Another point to be observed is the expression of a very human desire—the desire to pose as the inspired seer of coming events. Often have I seen scrawled announcements of the winners of races, big and small, a week or more before the meeting. And yet—another oddity— this desire to exhibit the gift of prophecy is not egotistical. For the prophet is always content to remain anonymous."

"Ah, sir, that's where you are not sufficiently wide-o."

"Wide-o?"

" I beg your pardon. I should say—not sufficiently hard-boiled."

" Hard-boiled ? "

" Er—well, not sufficiently informed on the stunts and rackets of these times."

" As how ? "

" Why, sir, so far from this being an expression of an Old Moore ambition, it has a base commercial object. Yes ; the names of those horses, none of which has an earthly, are written up as winners in the hope that simple punters, being of a superstitious cast, will take notice of them. The superstitious man, being suddenly confronted with the Writing on the Wall, regards it as a magical omen ; and if, as often happens, it links with some half-formed hunch of his own, he obeys it. That is what it's put there for—to lead him and his many mug-brothers to believe that somebody has inside information, which in turn leads him and the band of brothers to back the cripple, and thus do the bookies a bit of good."

"Indeed? The subtleties and pretences of modern life become more and more surprising to those, like myself, withdrawn from it. How right Longfellow was. Things really are not. I felt certain that it must be akin to the other scribblings — a release of some inhibited claim; in this case, to prognostication. But we are straying from our subject."

"Let us stray, sir. I am a natural vagrant. We were speaking of modern shyness in this matter, as against the eighteenth and earlier centuries. It's queer that in this age, which professes to admit everything, and to be outspoken as (it supposes) the Victorians never were, and to be emancipated from all prudery—it's queer that this shyness persists. Only a day or so ago, I was in a bar. The company were entirely men, and the staff were men. And a man came up to me, quite close, and whispered — he really did whisper :

'Can you tell me where's the lavatory ? ' ''

" Yes ; we have columns and volumes of talk about the facts of life, but the attitude seems to grow, as you say, more instead of less easy. In the smaller country hotels, such as I prefer to frequent when travelling, they are singularly reticent on the matter. Often I have tramped yards and yards of corridor, searching here and there, and finding it at last round some unsuspected corner, next to a cupboard where the staff keeps its brooms. In default of right-angled signs, visible down the corridor, they might at least tell one, when taking up one's bags, where it is. But they don't. And in some of these rambling, up-and-down places, even when one has found it once, one needs a plan, or a blazed trail, to find it again."

" Exactly, sir. It's just one of those

things that don't really exist. And to ask for it in a normal tone in the public lounge or the dining-room is to be marked as a barbarian—though perhaps secretly envied as one liberated. It has always puzzled me why, in some of the older railway stations, the place is disguised as Cloak Room. Granting the desire to disguise or hide it among the luggage, why was the luggage-room called Cloak Room ? Cloaks, to the best of my knowledge, were not worn after 1840 or so. And anyway, a traveller in one of those early and un-heated trains would surely wish to wear his top-coat rather than deposit it."

" Yes ; it is a point for consideration. It derives possibly from the coaching days when men sent their heavy cloaks ahead to the coach-office, where they could pick them up on boarding the coach. Or from the theatre, where the room was not only a place for the necessary deposit of cloaks, but a men's room generally."

" Despite what is believed to be the Victorian attitude, sir, I've noticed that in emergencies the older generation are more apt to name plainly what they want than those of my time."

" Quite, quite. I see that your studies have led you to realize that the tee-hee Strachey and his fellows are utterly at fault in their ideas of the Victorian age. They never can have read the popular journals of that period, or the social memoirs ; or indeed anything save *Our Life in the Highlands*, the *Leisure Hour*, the novels of Anthony Trollope, and *Home Life at Osborne House* ; all representing but a tiny fragment of the English scene and the English people. But let us have some more information, young man. Where, for example, do you experience least difficulty ? "

" Why, I should say in a district to which your life and affairs have probably kept you a stranger ; namely, South London, or that portion of it near the bridges. It is perhaps natural that one of the oldest bits of London should be well served in this matter— I mean the Borough High Street, the old road to and from Kent and Dover, and a busy thoroughfare in Stow's day and earlier. There, and around it, you have ample service, both open and concealed. Also in Waterloo Road, Blackfriars Road, and other parts. The great markets, too, are sure havens—Covent Garden ; Smithfield ; Billingsgate ; the Borough vegetable market—indeed all the labour quarters.

"And there you have a sociological sign-post. The frequency or infrequency of this service coincides curiously with local habits and regimen. Places are most frequent in those districts where there is large consumption of tea and beer ; least frequent in those districts where sherry and claret rule. You may deduce the one from the other."

"An interesting point. Now you mention it, I have noticed it. And in New York, where coffee is the staple drink—it is reflected there."

"It would be. Bearing these things in mind, it is advisable, after tea or Pilsner, so to arrange one's affairs that one does not get into the hinterland of Bayswater, or north of Regent's Park, or into the more westerly and unplumbed reaches of Cromwell Road."

"Cromwell Road — ha! Has any London explorer, do you know, reached its penetralia—discovered what lurks in its dusky curves west of the Natural History Museum—and returned to tell the tale?"

"Yes; I myself have. On just such an occasion as I have warned you against. A chill and forbidding road, and I paid dearly for my rashness. Had it not happened that its residential note is broken by a garage or two, I don't know. . . . But I did learn that that wounded snake of a road does at last come to a full stop—somewhere in the Fulham district."

" It is gratifying to know that. I have always had an uncanny feeling that it went on and on into a town something like London, but dimmer, dustier, spongier, and outside our dimensions. I used to fancy that the numerous cases of Mysterious Disappearance that we have in London were somehow connected with Cromwell Road. But continue."

" During day-time, of course, the museums of the Cromwell Road district are useful retreats. Indeed, in all parts of town, the museums, picture-galleries, and recreation grounds should be remembered. Also motor-coach stations. You spoke of churches offering service in some Continental towns; and it comes to me now that one London church does ; if not actually in its churchyard, at least alongside. I mean St. Paul's, Covent Garden."

" Well, that certainly shows an

advance from the prevailing attitude. We need more of the eighteenth-century honesty I spoke of. Though I do not, of course, go so far as to wish a return to the attitude of the seventeenth, or to such a restaurant scene as Dekker evokes in his *Gull's Hornbook*."

"I remember, sir. In the chapter on Behaviour in an Ordinary. Yes, far removed from prudery, and a good way towards brutality. Almost approaching in its tone the fireside conversation of Queen Elizabeth—as re-created in that curious little piece found locked away among the literary remains of Mark Twain."

"Ha! You know that remarkable bit of reconstruction, do you? Few copies, I believe, have got abroad. A knowledgeable young man, indeed. I shall begin to wonder what you don't know."

"Why, sir, you will remember that a wit of the 'nineties maintained that the young know everything."

"Yes, yes. A pity that no kind of

Pelmanism helps them to carry it to middle age."

"I should imagine, sir, that middle age has no need of certitude or omniscience. Its experience is taken for granted, and its opinions are listened to. Nobody challenges it, or sniffs at it, or tells it where it gets off, as they do with youth. Youth has to know everything, as defence against those elders who are constantly telling it how wrong it is. Last week I was challenged by a middle-aged man on that very province of knowledge which I have made my own. Because he had lived all his life in London, he claimed that he must know more about it than a man of half his age. And he asserted and protested that there was no service to be had within a furlong of St. James's Square. When I took him to Wells Street, and again from York Street into Mason's Yard, and effected introductions, he was decent enough to grunt. And for the rest of the afternoon he was willing to agree that I knew everything else—at least until five o'clock, always a testy hour with the middle-aged."

" But as you grow older, my boy, you will realize the difficulty of defining knowledge. At my age, I hesitate to say that I know anything. I did once know, but now I am not so sure. The aspect of things has a trick of going back on you, and what you once were sure was square flickers before your eyes as round. And what you once knew was *there* turns out to be *here*."

" I understand, sir. In this matter we are discussing I have once or twice found places which I have never been able to find again. I know they were not figments. I know they were solidly there, and as real as Kant allows anything to be. But somehow or other, though I have tried to recollect the turns I made, one to the right, then to the left, then through a passage, my feet have never recaptured the ritual steps that directed me originally. I do not doubt their existence, but I cannot assert it."

" I know. And doubtless you have found places where you never sought because you never believed they could be."

" Occasionally, yes. That is one of London's many charms—one is so often running against the unexpected and the incongruous. As in the case of St. Paul's, Covent Garden. I have found them—usually when they didn't interest me—in corners where nobody, save those whose way to and from home took them through that labyrinth of courts, or perhaps some errant and aimless circumambulator like myself, could possibly have found them. For example, in South Bruton Mews, which is off Hay Hill, which is off Berkeley Street. As a point for idle reflection, one can usually judge, from the district one is in, what kind of place one will find, or vice versa. A plain metal affair, metal throughout, belongs to a district of poor shops and houses, and low rates. Brown stone or porcelain, with work by Doulton, or Adamsez or Twyford's, or Davis and Bennett, denotes a well-to-do district. Though the finest things of this kind that I have seen anywhere, I saw, not in London, but in the state-controlled houses of Carlisle."

"Very likely. Very likely. That is why, though my mind tells me that Socialism is right, my being withholds confirmation. Socialism, it seems, is always so concerned with hygiene and disinfectant, with the matter of fact, and the thing rather than the image, that it will have little time or place for the graces and *décor* and follies that give life its pungency or perfume. Life is something more than biology and anthropology. It needs a certain amount of litter. And, of course, it needs its cherry-blossom, as in the short story of that Soviet writer, whose name escapes me, though I remember the story."

" I too. It concerned a love affair, which the man wished to be a plain affair of mating, while the girl was un-modern enough to want to dress the room with flowers."

" Yes. That is the flaw in all these worlds that are presented as ideal. Attention to the trivial necessity, and neglect of the important auxiliary. Everything made tidy for creatures who reach their fullest realization when untidy. Material things clean and bright for people who notice only whether a place is comfortable, and whether the company have bright minds."

" True, sir. Though on our general subject I have heard that men are sometimes affected by surroundings. Indeed, I have heard of men becoming seriously indisposed in small Conti-nental towns by the reaction upon their minds of the arrangements for necessary affairs."

" That may be. Still, I am of my generation. I do not belong to this age, and I can live the rest of my days without steel furniture, or hygienic dishes, or sun-parlours on the roof ; and I can satisfy all needs without chromium fittings in the bathroom and kindred places. I grew up in an age of bed-socks and night-caps and closed windows, and rough-and-ready sanitation, and I don't know that I'm much the worse. Anyway, 'tis a fact that I've reached the age of seventy-seven, and if I were not running the risk of being called a boastful old fool, I would point to that age, and to greater ages reached by many of us Mid-Victorians. Ages which I take leave to doubt will be reached by many of the present nervous generation, with its morbid concern over its health, and its hygiene, and its diet, and its Keeping Fit. Healthy people *are* fit, and they never

think or talk about it. And being
healthy has little to do with the things
that medical men and sanitary officers
make so much of. You, my boy, seem
more sensible than most of the morbid
young fellows around here. Perhaps
you feel fit to—er—what is it—Knock
Back another ? "

" In my stride, sir."

" Well, now, with your remarkable
knowledge (another Pilsner, Henry), I
suppose if I were to name any spot of
London, you could tell me at once
the nearest place to that spot. Even
if it were Kensington or St. John's
Wood, you could no doubt name the
nearest."

" Almost, I believe. . . . Yet another
kind love, sir. A-a-ah ! "

" Victoria Street, then ? "

" Victoria Street ? Well, if you have
left the bottom of Parliament Street,
where the subway has provision, the
only obvious place is at the other end,
at the corner of Vauxhall Bridge Road.

But at about the middle you have two side-street places. Turn into Broadway, on the right, and you find full service, with silver railings, outside Transport House. Farther down, about opposite the Army and Navy Stores, you can turn into Buckingham Gate, alongside the Albert Tavern, and you will find a place hidden behind two clearly visible telephone-booths."

"Useful. And Soho and Shaftesbury Avenue — though I seldom visit that district."

"Why, for Shaftesbury Avenue, you have at one end the Piccadilly Circus subway, and in the middle a visible place in Cambridge Circus, fronting the Palace Theatre. For the invisible, you need only go a few steps down Macclesfield Street, and turn into Dansey Place. For Soho, a yard or two up Wardour Street, beyond Old Compton Street, brings you to a narrow passage opposite Pulteney Street. Or you may go up Berwick Street, and turn into Broad Street, where you will find full service."

" And Holborn, where I occasionally find myself after seeing my solicitor ? "

" Why, you have service outside the Holborn Empire, and just by the Prudential Insurance office. Between those points, if need be, you can go up Featherstone Buildings, and you will see a place facing you at the top. If your business was at the Theobald's Road end of Gray's Inn, you may come out there, and alongside you will find a street called Jockey's Fields, which has an enclosure a few yards from the road. Or full service across Gray's Inn Road at the junction of Clerkenwell Road and Rosebery Avenue."

" Encyclopaedic, young man. John Stow in his *Survey* was not more vigilant and curious."

" I mentioned some places to be avoided after tea. Others are—Euston Road (from Tottenham Court Road to King's Cross); Holland Park Avenue ;

Grosvenor Road ; Baker Street (from Marylebone Road to Oxford Street) ; Victoria Embankment—save at either end ; the Mall and Constitution Hill ; Bond Street ; Kensington Road (from High Street to Olympia) ; Brompton Road ; and Chelsea Embankment. There are others, but those are all that occur to me at the moment. You will have a shorter search in Paris for a restaurant with a tobacco licence, than you will have in those streets for the needful. In certain circumstances it is exasperating to see, at points of some of them, minatory notices concerning nuisance, without any direction as to where one may go so as to be in order. By the way, while I think of it, beware also of visiting—which, I imagine, sir, you are hardly likely to do—any of those new suburbs on the outskirts. Unless you are sure of yourself."

" No ; I cannot conceive any change in my affairs or entourage that would be likely to involve my presence at those appalling disfigurements of London's green. Though, of course, people must live somewhere. The pity is that wherever they are, there is always some over-developed egotist like myself who wishes they would live somewhere else. But I feel that about most people of any sort—about the majority of the members here. And I fancy each of them feels that way about the rest of us. No doubt many sensitive souls in Brighthelmstone felt that way about George and his Pavilion. They did not begrudge him his amusement, but would have preferred him to have it at any other spot of the coast. And no doubt when proposals are made to afford public service to man by the establishment of a green enclosure, numerous protests are received from those living near the spot."

"As to that, sir, I cannot say. It may explain why the streets I have named are so apparently thoughtless."

"It would be interesting to know who decides when and where such a place shall be opened. Is it petitioned by those having daily occasion to use the thoroughfare, do you think? And perhaps, as I say, cross-petitioned by the residents? With a casting vote for the chairman? Or is it left to the whimsy of some departmental chief, who, on a morning when he has nothing to do, looks around certain quarters of London and decides that they need an addition to their amenities? Or perhaps finds that the department has a large stock of fittings that have been a long time in store, and is suddenly moved to scatter them about the town indiscriminately?"

"I should think the latter, since one's observation affords no sign of a standard or plan. Often one finds four close together, and then nothing for a mile. It is possible that before they do anything they set watchers on the spot they are considering. Like those traffic watchers one sees, who stand in doorways with note-books, counting the buses and other vehicles and writing down cryptic figures."

"Does one see them? I never have. Do they really count the buses—and what for? It sounds a tedious and exhausting occupation, needing a swift eye."

"It does. As to why they do it, I cannot say. I have twice asked, in my most engaging manner, but each time I was told to . . . but that is neither here nor there. I will only say that I can do that kind of thing too, and that I left the man looking pale and distraught. . . . As I was saying, it is possible that they set watchers on an ill-served spot, and that the watchers over a period of days note the number of pedestrians passing that barren spot. And if the number is large, it is decided that the spot shall have a place. But in the result it may be that the watchers, either by reason of rain or blunt pencils, find their figures undecipherable, or get them mixed, and so, as I think, recommend putting one on a spot already served, and negative the proposal where one is badly needed. But I don't really know. I am just indulging in conjecture. The whole matter is wrapped in that obscurity in which the English prefer to leave it."

" There is, I believe, a public gallery at the County Hall, from which ordinary people like ourselves may listen to the proceedings. Probably a visit to a sessions of the Sanitary Department would make the whole thing clear."

" Maybe it would, sir. And yet, despite my occasional irritation at what sometimes appears to be a lack of plan and consideration, I don't know that I want it made clear. I have some streak of the poet. I dislike exchanging the shadow of fancy for the bone of reality. I prefer to let my mind play around the mystery, as it plays around

[57]

the mystery of radio, and the mystery of why the two o'clock from Euston to Birmingham always has a certain number of passengers. One would think that there might be one day in the year when nobody wanted to go from London to Birmingham at two o'clock. But there isn't. And this matter is equally mysterious. During my little life in London—not long, but full of hours and each hour used for observation, I have never seen a green enclosure being erected, or an underground place being tunnelled for. How it's done I don't know. I thought at first it must be done at dead of night, and that in some way the work was camouflaged during daylight hours as telephone work or repaving. But I've been about London at all hours between midnight and six, and have seen nothing of the kind going on. Maybe they are done by the earth-dwellers—gnomes, brown people, little red men, Robin Goodfellows. Anyway, I've never seen them at it. And when they *are* built, they just appear on the scene. Never does the local mayor ' open ' them, as he opens public baths and wash-houses and playing-fields and hospitals."

" It should be done," said Mr. Mumble. " And when once done, it would put an end to the grins or embarrassment which, as we all know, are often caused in certain circles by mention of these places. Who, I wonder, will be the pioneer mayor in this matter ? He will be subject, of course, to considerable criticism from some quarters, and ribaldry from others. But the common denominator of feeling, I think, will applaud his common sense. Your little street-plans, if you can get them on the market, should help. And perhaps in time they will appear in every London guide and directory. They might even become a valuable property to you, like the Buff Guide or the Red Book or Wisden. A new issue annually, with latest additions and a note of obsolete or abandoned places. With a preface by the Minister of Health, and critical or constructive articles by advanced experts in sanitary matters."

" That is an idea, sir. I shall consider it and see how best to exploit it."

" There should be a place for it among a wide public. After all, in these days there are guides to all manner of things. Strange things. On a station bookstall last week I noticed, for example, a Guide to the Pools. An odd work to prepare, and I hardly see the need for it. A Guide to the Lakes, yes ; but the Pools . . . what pools have we ? The Silent Pool, at Shere ; Frensham Ponds ; the Swan Pool at Abbotsbury."

" I think, sir, the pools in question are——"

" And the other day I saw a Guide to the Best Films. As if there were any. But a year or so ago I did see a quite useful Guide ; one that must have had a considerable sale. It was a Guide to Avoiding Payment of Debt."

" Useless, I fear, to me, sir, since I can never find anybody who will allow me to contract it. But perhaps when my street-plans get going, some of the West End establishments will be encouraged to invite me into their ledgers. I have noticed with the better kind of shop that it doesn't seem to want your actual money. It only wants to know that you've got plenty. If you have, you can run on for a year or more."

" Well, my boy, go ahead with your plans ; get them out for the tourist season, and I warrant you will soon have plenty. And, by the way, you might remember to include a note which may or may not have occurred to you. The point has come under my own observation, and I pass it on. It is this : that many foreigners, unfamiliar with the structure of our places, often enter the shelters at our taxi-ranks under a wholly mistaken notion of their purpose. Sometimes this contretemps helps to strengthen the *entente cordiale* and the comity of nations ; at other times it does not. You could assist them in the matter with a couple of little designs."

" That, sir, is a useful point that I had not foreseen. I will certainly embody it. And as in these days of swift transport we receive visitors from all countries, do you happen to know the prevailing design in China, Iraq, the Isles of Greece, New Guinea, Uruguay, Madagascar, and Sumatra ? "

" I confess I do not."

" I was thinking that the people of these various countries, according to their national design, might make more startling mistakes than taxi-shelters, and blunder into places where the matter would not be so easily righted."

" As, for example . . . ? "

" Well, Broadcasting House — the

tramcar subway at Victoria Embankment—the keepers' lodges at the park gates—the Albert Memorial—the sentries' arches at the Horse Guards—Burlington Arcade — Albany — Tattersall's.''

" Yes, that is possible. We are all prone to mistakes, but foreigners' mistakes always seem more curious than our own. The Englishman who, on a first visit to Bruges, wrote home that the train ran right into the church, may perhaps be pardoned. And even those Englishmen who, on a first visit, mistake the purpose of the foot-bath that one finds in the bedrooms of small French hotels. But I cannot see similar excuse for the American actress whose acquaintance I enjoyed for a brief while. Going to a Bond Street establishment for some purchase, she saw on the door the Royal arms and the words By Appointment, and went elsewhere, explaining that she could not bother with those places where you

[63]

had to write first. Nor can I see justi-
fication for the Maltese visitor I heard
of, who went up and down in a Tube
lift a dozen times before he ventured
to ask how many more stops before
Regent's Park. But I can easily see
that Broadcasting House in its white
austerity might be mistaken for many
things—a dairy, perhaps, or a crema-
torium.''

    '' To me, sir, it suggests less credible
things than those. . . . But somehow or
other I must certainly find out about
the designs in remote countries. There
is India, for example. An elderly friend
of mine, an architect, once received
a commission for a theatre for some
Indian city. He designed what he
thought was a posh and practical building, giving clear views of the stage
from all parts, and with retiring rooms
for Ladies and Gentlemen—one on each
side of the house. He submitted his
plans and received them back, with
instructions to pull the thing to pieces

and re-design it, with three retiring rooms on each side. He had forgotten, or did not know, about the creeds and castes of India, or that those of one creed may not use a place used by those of another."

" Yet we have reflections of the same thing here," said Mr. Mumble. " In my own short wanderings outside my regular district, I have noticed differences. In some parts—probably the more democratic parts—the places we are speaking of are notified by the heroic word Men. While all round this district we see only the word Gentlemen. And I believe a similar distinction is observed in Army barracks, where the grand and epic term is reserved for the creature regarded as the lowest."

"Paradoxical and pointless, sir, to my thinking. Differences are absolute or non-existent. They cannot be created by uniforms or possessions or other artificial means. Particularly in this matter which, in its occurrence, brings all men to equality. In Europe this is recognized, and on those occasions all men, whatever their actual or artificial rank, are named as members of the genus Homo."

" I appreciate that. I am myself by no means a democrat, but I perceive the poetic justice of accepting man's common structure in certain situations without distinction. As in hospitals where, after a motor smash, peer and pauper lose their worldly differences and become organisms in a society of one class called Cases, so in this other matter we should all be Men. . . . But by the movement in the hall it appears to be lunch-time. Tables will be filling up. Since you have endured my maundering thus far, perhaps you will join my table and continue to instruct me."

" My natural conceit permits me to believe that on this one subject I can. On all others I would gladly listen to you, sir, and I accept your kind invitation in the assurance that I shall benefit not only by a pleasant meal but by the fruit of a well-stored mind."

"Thank you, my boy. If Spain were not at this moment engaged in what is paradoxically called a civil war, I should describe your courtesy as something more than Castilian. But in these times that would be a meiosis. Is it innate or did you acquire it under some modern Henry Peachum?"

"Partly innate, sir, derived from my father, who was a wine-merchant, and from *his* father, who was a captain of rustic militia. And partly a second nature grafted upon me by the exigencies of trying to sell tap-washers to traders who had no demand for them."

"Ha. Then it has a stout spine. Well, you have given me some useful information, and I hope I shall remember it. But perhaps if I book a table, you could recapitulate, and I could take a note."

"With pleasure, sir. . . . Supposing we ignore the City, which is a small area, and start from, say, Ludgate Circus. Taking the main and visible stations from that point, which has one itself, we proceed up Fleet Street, and find a station at the foot of Fetter Lane. Then, between the Law Courts and St. Clement Danes. Then at Wellington Street, approaching Waterloo Bridge. Then Charing Cross Station or the Trafalgar Square subway. Also at the bottom of Villiers Street in Embankment Gardens. Then Charing Cross Road, by the Garrick Theatre. Then Leicester Square. Then Piccadilly Circus subway. Then Oxford Circus. And near it, Great Marlborough Street. Then Green Park gate by the Ritz. (Am I going too fast?) West of Piccadilly you have Hyde Park Corner, at the Park entrance, and Knightsbridge, by Brompton Road. Also the Park entrance by Marble Arch. North of Piccadilly you have Cambridge Circus, outside the Palace Theatre ; New Oxford Street, where it meets Bloomsbury High Street ; and the end of Shaftesbury Avenue, facing Prince's Theatre. The Holborn places I have mentioned—outside the Holborn Empire and outside the Prudential Insurance building. Also the place at Newgate Street, outside the Old Bailey. At Smithfield a place will be found in the open space fronting Bart's Hospital, and in Farringdon Street just at the foot of Charterhouse Street. Tottenham Court Road has provision outside Warren Street Station, and Euston Road at the junction with Great Portland Street. Marylebone Road, just opposite Tussaud's. Kensington High Street, in a sidewalk by the Town Hall. Sloane Square, in that space fronting the Court Theatre.

" So much for the open stations of the main streets—a dull recitative, I fear. As for the concealed places, some of which have been named in our talk, they would make a list ten times as long, an aria to the recitative, but so scattered up and down the map that one needs a coloratura to sing them. But I shall dot them all on my little plans."

"Thank you, my boy. I've got all the main ones down. And now, let us see if there's anything fit to eat."

"Right, sir. If you will excuse me one moment. Those two——"

"Certainly. I'm coming that way too. Lead on, my boy. Luckily, we're in the club and not in St. John's Wood."

"Rather, sir. Though if it were still a wood it would be a less troublesome spot. In that connection, I recall a story. It concerns one of the elder artists of the district who, fearing to be left behind, had forcibly converted himself to surréalisme. Being one night——"

" Don't tell me now, my boy. Keep
it for the hors d'œuvre. The things
they serve in this place need some
condiment. Lead on, my boy, lead
on. . . ."